BITTERSWEET

12 SHORT STORIES FOR MODERN LIFE

JULIE STOCK

CLUED UP PUBLISHING

Cover Design: Oliphant Publishing Services

To anyone who has ever struggled, and survived.

1

THE HUSTLE

'May I?'

I looked up to see a man gesturing at the chair next to me, empty except for my black flight bag. His tanned, weathered face was covered with stubble and his spiky hair had been dyed an odd shade of yellow.

'Of course!' I replied, moving the bag to the floor and trying not to stare at his dishevelled appearance.

I returned to reading my Kindle as the man sat down heavily in the chair next to me, folding his tall body into the tiny seat. I heard him heave a large sigh as he deposited a well-worn, black leather holdall at his feet.

'At least you've got something to read while we wait,' he said, running his hand over his face.

I looked up and nodded. 'I have lots of books on here actually,' I said, ignoring the advice in my head about not letting myself be drawn into conversation with a stranger, 'which is great for situations like this.' I smiled as his incongruous, black eyebrows shot up.

'How many books does that device hold then?'

'I think they can hold about a thousand.'

He nodded. 'I've had so many delays on this trip, as well as losing my luggage, I could have done with something like that to help me while away the hours.'

And there it was. The invitation.

'What happened to you?' I asked.

His eyes lit up as he told me the story of all the delays on his trip to Taiwan, via innumerable countries on endless continents and the misery of losing his luggage. Suddenly, the delay for our flight to London didn't seem so bad. I nodded wisely, commiserating with him about the difficulties of modern travel. He fell silent and didn't look at me again so I returned to my reading, thinking the conversation was over.

About ten minutes later, he stood up again.

'Well, I'm off to get a coffee.' He pronounced it *cawfee* and I smiled at how foreign that accent still sounded to my ears, even after so many years of travelling to and from the States.

'Good talking to you,' I replied.

I watched him for a moment as he ambled off swinging his bag at his side and made his way towards the café nearby. I started reading once again but I couldn't concentrate. The next time I looked up, there was no sign of him.

Just then, the tannoy announced that our flight was finally boarding.

I'd been in the queue for about five minutes when out of the corner of my eye, I sensed someone approaching me.

'Excuse me, madam, is this your bag?' An airport official was standing over me now pointing at my bag on the floor.

'Yes.'

'Come with me, please.'

'What's this about?' I asked as the official picked up my bag. 'I can't come with you, I'll miss my flight,' I said.

'I'm afraid that's the least of your worries, madam.' He grasped my elbow and steered me towards a white door. I had no idea what lay behind it but I had an ominous feeling that it wouldn't be good.

I found myself in a plain white room with just a table and some chairs in it. On one side, there were two chairs and one of them was occupied by another airport official. This one was a woman. Her arms were crossed and her face was devoid of all expression. The man who'd brought me in gestured towards the empty chair on the other side of the table. He sat down next to the stony-faced woman and after a moment's hesitation, I took my place across from them. I straightened my skirt and waited to hear what they had to say.

The man lifted my bag on to the table. 'Shall we have a look inside here and check whether this is your bag?'

'Sure,' I replied, unsure as to why they thought it wasn't my bag. 'Oh hang on, you'll need the key for the padlock. I always lock the central compartment.'

I reached into my handbag to find the tiny key.

'There's no padlock on the bag, ma'am.'

I looked up sharply, staring at the bag. The black flight bag on the table was subtly different to my own. I stood up in my panic. The official had already unzipped the main compartment. It was full of men's clothes, as well as some toiletries, books and men's health magazines. It was clearly not my bag. I leaned over to check the other side of the bag, still not wanting to believe this was happening to me. My bag had two pockets on the outside. That's where I usually stored my passport and other flight documents for easy access. There were no pockets. I sank into my seat, feeling the blood drain from my face.

'This isn't my bag even though it looks very similar.' I paused for a moment. 'That man with the yellow hair. He sat down next to me in the waiting area and he had a black bag as well. It's all coming back to me now. God, my bag has my passport in it as well.'

The female official stood up then and abruptly left the room.

'Why didn't you notice that he'd taken your bag?'

'As I said, he had a black flight bag as well so I probably just didn't see him do it. I obviously wasn't expecting him to take my bag. How did you even know that this had happened?'

'A passenger sitting opposite you noticed when the man with the yellow hair picked up your bag rather than his own when he left, and he reported it to us as being suspicious.'

I sat back in my chair shocked by what had happened and wondering what I was going to do if I had lost my passport. I had no doubt that the man would be long gone by now.

The female official returned a few minutes later carrying my almost identical black flight bag. She set it down on the table next to the other one and reached into one of the front pockets. I breathed a sigh of relief as she pulled out my passport and handed it to me to check.

'Thank God,' I gushed. 'He must have taken my bag by mistake when he left me.'

'We'll be following that up, ma'am. We found him sitting some-where else at the same gate so we've brought him in for questioning as well. He did seem as surprised as you were by what had happened.'

'Am I free to go now then?'

'Yes, ma'am you are. Please take good care of your luggage from this point on. If you're quick, you might just make that flight to London after all.'

Once the flight had taken off for London and I knew I was safely on my way, I stood up to retrieve my flight bag so that I could check the contents for myself. The officials had given me the padlock at the airport and I'd decided not to use it as I no longer needed it now. I confirmed that everything that should be there was definitely in the bag, but I was also pleased to see the new item that Jerry had dropped in there for me while he was temporarily in possession of my bag. I smiled. The black velvet bag was small and inconspicuous so the officials probably wouldn't even have noticed it if they'd done a search. I opened it the tiniest fraction within my bag so that no-one else would see. Once I confirmed the diamond necklace was inside the bag, I pulled the drawstring closed quickly and re-zipped the flight bag. I sat back down again after stowing the bag in the overhead locker.

Jerry had turned the diamonds into a necklace for me in just one day since the robbery at the jeweller's store in Manhattan. No-one would know the necklace was so valuable nor that we had managed to get the diamonds out of the country so easily. Once I was in Europe again, I'd break the necklace back up and sell the diamonds one at a time to foreign dealers and no-one would be any the wiser.

They wouldn't be able to hold Jerry for long at the airport. He would just say he had picked up my bag by mistake and as I'd got everything back, it would lend weight to his claims of innocence. I chuckled to myself as I thought about his yellow hair – it had been distinctive enough to get him noticed as we'd planned – but he'd hated it nevertheless. By the time he joined me in Paris when we had the funds, it would have grown out and we could go unnoticed in the city once again.

2

MIDDLE EIGHT

Josie stared at her notepad willing inspiration to strike so she could finish the final eight bars of her song. She'd been staring at the paper for several hours now and still had nothing to go with, not a single note, let alone a bar. She threw the pad down on the table in front of her and stood up, stretching out the kinks that had developed in her neck as a result of sitting in the same position since lunchtime – hunched over with her hand poised above the page for when the first seed of an idea appeared.

She was parched after spending so many hours working. She made her way to her kitchenette and poured herself a long, tall glass of water from the fridge before downing it in one. It was a steamy hot summer's day and she'd been stupid not to rehydrate herself throughout the afternoon. That was the last thing she needed when she was due in the recording studio first thing tomorrow to start laying down the tracks for her new album.

She'd never experienced a block like this before. She'd written a catchy chorus and several verses which told her story so well but just couldn't find the contrast needed for the eight bars that would make up the bridge. She wanted lyrics as well as chords, and although she had some ideas for minor chords, she simply couldn't find the words to say what was on her mind. She usually had no problem deepening the emotional impact of her songs in those middle eight bars; in fact, she thrived on it. Perhaps she was losing her touch. She looked wistfully at her battered old acoustic guitar. She loved it like a member of her own family. It had seen her through all the good times, as well as the bad. But today the magic was missing.

She decided to go out for some air. Maybe she just needed some time to think away from her notepad, her guitar and the confines of her small apartment. She picked up her purse and keys, slipped on her sunglasses and headed out.

She made her way down to the river bank, her favourite place to think when she was struggling musically. She sat down on the scorched grass and stared out at the water bubbling over the rocks on the river bed. The flow of the water soothed her spirit and her eyelids began to droop as the calm washed over her. She lay back on the grass, looking up at the cloudless sky – such a beautiful day. In no time she was asleep. The next thing she knew, something wet was nudging her arm and as she came to, shielding her eyes from the afternoon sun, she saw a small dog had appeared next to her.

'Hey, where'd you come from?' She reached out her hand and the dog sniffed it and gave her a lick, encouraging her to stroke his sleek, red coat.

'Brandy! Where've you gone, boy?'

A man emerged from behind a tree and stopped in front of her. His intense, dark-brown eyes appraised her and her cheeks heated under his scrutiny.

'Hi there. Is this your dog?' She went for the friendly stranger approach, rather than 'I was about to kidnap your dog and you caught me.'

'Sure is. I'm sorry he bothered you.' The man smiled revealing a set of almost startling white teeth.

'No bother, he's lovely. Brandy, was it?'

'Yep, not very original, I'm afraid.' They both laughed then. 'Well, I'll let you get back to your day. Bye.'

Josie watched as he went on his way with his energetic little dog, and she missed their company at once. She sighed and stood up, brushing the grass off her dress, keen to get back and see whether the time she'd spent by the riverside had offered her any inspiration. The air grew heavy as she made her way home, a sure sign rain was on the way. As she approached her apartment block, she felt the first raindrop and picked up speed to avoid getting drenched when the inevitable downpour came. She ran the last few yards but when the raindrops fell, it was so refreshing to feel the water on her skin that she stopped, allowing the rain to soak into her. She turned her face up to the now overcast sky and gave herself to the elements.

Josie was up early and into the recording studio long before she expected anyone else to be there. She'd brought her guitar with her so she could do her final practice on her own. By the time the sound engineers and the rest of the band turned up, she was more than ready to start laying down the tracks for her album.

'Hey, Josie, how's it going?' Her manager was the most positive person she'd ever met and whatever her mood, he was always upbeat.

'I'm so good today, Brad, you won't believe it when you hear,' she replied with a conspiratorial grin.

'D'you finish that final song you've been struggling with?'

'Sure did.'

'Well, I can't wait to hear it.'

The morning passed quickly as they laid down the songs telling the story of her life. By lunchtime, Josie was tired but happy with the progress they'd made. She went to speak to Jed, the chief sound engineer, to see what he thought of what they'd done so far.

'You should be real proud, Josie. You sound fantastic out there. Yours is one of the best début albums I've ever heard.'

She blushed at Jed's praise. She must have really earned it for him to speak so highly of her work. She touched him lightly on the arm to convey her thanks, and went back to the live room to lay down the final tracks. They'd made a conscious decision to go with the first take of each track without revising it at this stage. They'd listen back to the album as a whole before deciding whether to make any changes.

It was finally time to sing the final track, the one she'd struggled with for so many days – until she'd met Brandy and his owner. She'd been so hung up on finding the right words for her middle eight but as Brandy had come bounding into view, the burbling river providing the backdrop to her story, she'd realised that words weren't necessary. Her guitar did the rest, and although it had taken her most of the previous night to note it down, she'd known in her heart that she'd cracked it. She only hoped Brad agreed with her. As she played the last note, she looked up into his eyes. When he didn't give any indication of his feelings, she glanced over at Jed, before looking round at the rest of the band. Silence. Silence, followed by rapturous applause.

'That one's a winner, Josie. For sure.' Brad beamed at her and so did everyone else. She made a mental note to return to the river the next day to thank Brandy... and his owner.

3

A RANDOM ACT OF KINDNESS

John sits on his favourite bench in the park, waiting for the shops to close. It's already dark, although it's only late afternoon. Winter surrounds him. He shivers, his clothing offering him little protection against the plummeting temperatures. He glances at the sleeping bag rolled up on the bench next to him, his only possession apart from the clothes he's wearing. He takes a drink from the half-empty can of cheap cider, which was all he'd been able to afford with what he'd collected today. Food would warm him up more but food is a luxury now.

He watches the shoppers dashing to and fro snapping up last-minute Christmas presents, and wishes that Christmas is as high on his priority list as it is on theirs. A memory of his children's happy faces flashes through his mind, first Rosie, then Jack. They loved Christmas, of course. Jack had only managed to experience two Christmases before their whole world had come to an abrupt end. John closes his eyes, willing the memories to leave him alone but the flashbacks to the night when the lorry had crashed into Stella's car still haunt him.

The lights are still on in the bookshop but he knows it can't be long now. He used to love books but he can't imagine ever being able to lose himself in one again. The blonde-haired girl from the bookshop closes up at last and turns off the lights. Recognising his cue, he makes his way across the street and positions himself in the doorway, sideways on to the street so that the more inquisitive passersby can't catch his eye.

Wrapped in his sleeping bag, he dozes, visions of his lost family crowding his mind. He shudders and a hacking cough wracks his weakened body. He feels someone shake him gently and as he opens his eyes, he looks up into the face of the blonde-haired girl. It is full of kindness, not pity.

'Would you like a cup of tea or coffee?' She smiles gently at him, her blonde hair framing her face like an angel.

He shakes his head. He doesn't want to go inside. She goes back into the shop and he misses that offer of a drink at once. A few minutes later, she brings a drink outside to him instead. Then she leaves.

Sadie makes another hot drink for the homeless man, now resident every night for a full week in the doorway outside her shop. The wary look in his eyes is still there and probably never goes away.

'By the way, I'm Sadie,' she tells him as she hands him his drink tonight. His eyebrows raise a fraction but still, he says nothing. She hovers next to him, summoning up the courage to continue. 'The shop will be closing early tomorrow with it being Christmas Eve.' A frown crosses the man's face and she rushes on, desperate to reassure him. 'I'll be helping out at the soup kitchen down at St. Andrew's though. We open at six and it's free if you want to come along.'

Sadie steps back and says no more, not wanting to push the man against his will. She retreats into the shop, turns the lights off and makes her way home. She's wrapped up warm against the biting wind; thick padded coat, woollen scarf and hat, as well as thermal gloves and still the cold creeps inside her defences. At least she's luckier than those poor homeless people sleeping on the street. If only she could do more to help them. She determines to speak to the vicar at the church again the next day to see whether they can work together to start a night shelter. Ever since reading about one in a nearby town, she's been trying to encourage the local council to work together with charities and churches in the area to provide a regular service for homeless people, helping them to rebuild their lives. But no-one's listening so far. She won't give up though. She knows only too well how life can change in a split second, and she wants to make sure no-one else suffers like her brother did. Her grief is not as painful now but she often thinks about how lonely he must have been at the end, how desperate he must have been for someone to care, even a stranger.

John debates whether to go along to the church all the next day but in the end, his hunger wins out. When he pushes open the door of the ancient building, the inside is full of people and the warmth caresses his face. Desperate times, he thinks. He even sees people he knows from the street and they nod cautiously at each other. He joins the queue of people shuffling along to collect their soup. He sees Sadie serving people with a smile.

'We're here again tomorrow on Christmas Day, don't forget,' he hears her tell someone in front of him. 'Tell anyone else you know who's living on the street and struggling. It's a full meal tomorrow and everyone's welcome.'

John finds the kindness a little overwhelming. He wonders how all the others got into this state. He never would have taken the time to consider it before. He hadn't been a cruel man, just an unseeing one, like most other people who've never suffered such indignity. If he had his time again, he'd be more mindful about how many people were living on the streets, he'd try and do something about it, something to make a difference, like Sadie... but then he checks himself, knowing that none of that is true. He was too self-centred back then, too wrapped up in his own life to care about anyone else's. And he thanks goodness for Sadie and the other helpers in the church for the kindness they're showing to people like him.

Too many people turn a blind eye, just like he did. What kind of a society is that?

4

_____

THE EYE OF THE BEHOLDER

James studied the display of jewellery through the shop window, rubbing absently at his temples while staring through the glass. The array of engagement rings available was overwhelming: solitaires, clusters, modern and traditional. How on earth was he going to choose the one for Talia? He'd been dating her for just over a year, and although he loved her, she'd become more and more demanding, criticising him at every turn.

She'd made it clear she would expect to have the best available if he should ever ask her to marry him, so there was no way he could go for the budget choice. He groaned and closed his eyes briefly, dreading how much this was going to set him back. His salary didn't stretch to such frivolous purchases. He would probably have to eat bread and water for the next few months to claw the money back.

On the other side of the glass, a salesman had appeared, smiling at him and beckoning him inside. There was no way out now. The bell tinkled as the door closed behind him.

'Hello, sir. How can I help you today?'

James struggled to form a sentence that would explain his dilemma without making him look like a cheapskate.

'I'm looking for an engagement ring. I want to buy something special but within my budget.'

'I see.'

The man rubbed his hands together and licked his lips before nodding at James. 'Of course, sir. I have just the thing.' He took James by the elbow and guided him over to a display of vintage rings, the ones in the window long since forgotten. James' eyes were drawn immediately to a solitaire diamond ring with a twisted band clasping the glittering stone in its centre. He was convinced Talia would love it as much as he did.

'What the hell is this? You are joking, right?'

James looked up at Talia's contorted face from his kneeling position on the floor of the restaurant in which he'd chosen to propose. Silence fell around the room and he swallowed, unsure of what to say next. He stood up slowly, trying not to lose his balance. He took a step towards his girlfriend but she threw her hand up warding him off.

'If you think I'm wearing this monstrosity, you're sadly mistaken.' She snapped the lid of the black velvet box shut and shoved it across the table away from her.

'Talia, I'm sorry, I can get you a different ring...'

'No. You clearly know nothing about me. This is over.' With that, she stood up, picked up her bag and jacket, and left the restaurant, leaving James to face his shame alone.

All he could think about was the £500 the vintage ring had cost him and now she wasn't even going to wear it. Thank goodness he'd proposed before they'd ordered any food. He threw a couple of notes onto the table, grabbed his jacket and left the scene of his embarrassment behind him.

Outside on the street, the sun was shining and he realised he'd had a lucky escape. His shoulders relaxed and the pounding in his head began to ease.

He stood across the road for several minutes, weighing up whether he was brave enough to enter the dingy looking establishment tucked in between a launderette and a kebab shop. At last, he breathed in deeply and crossed the busy high street. The bell tinkled as the door closed behind him. He walked up to the counter and bent slightly to look through the grille at the older man on the other side.

'What can I help you with today?' The man didn't even look up from the work he was doing.

James took the velvet box out of his jacket pocket and passed it underneath the bars.

The man put his work to one side, his attention drawn by the prospect of what was in the box. He opened the box and then gave James a long look before taking out a loupe to study the ring more closely. He looked at it from every angle before looking James in the eye once more.

'Are you looking to pawn it or sell it?'

'To sell it.' James blew out a long breath but said no more.

'Where did you get it?' The man looked suspicious, and James hurried to explain.

'Can you hang on a moment? I need to check something out back.'

The man shuffled through a door at the rear of his tiny work-space, his dirty old cardigan swinging behind him, and disappeared.

James wiped his hands on his jeans, wishing he'd never come in this place, yet acutely aware that he couldn't have gone back to the oily salesman at the shop either. A clock on the wall ticked loudly as the seconds went by.

'I'm sorry but I can't buy this ring from you,' the man said as he reappeared. He passed the velvet box under the grille once more together with a folded sheet of paper. 'I'm doing you a favour, man. You look like you could use a break.'

James took the box and the sheet, and left the shop, confused by all that had just happened. He walked away down the street before ducking into a doorway to read the piece of paper. He gasped as he recognised Talia's ring in the photo at the top of the sheet.

'£5,000 *reward offered for stolen vintage ring. Sentimental value. Please contact me on the number below in strict confidence.*'

5

THE INTRUDER

Maya stared out the window at the garden, marvelling at the number of birds flying past. Their beauty never failed to amaze her. A noise caught her attention and she turned her head slowly to see what it was.

'Hey, beautiful. How are you this morning?' Sarah stroked her head and she leaned into her caress.

Maya heard Sarah pottering about in the kitchen preparing food and singing along to the radio in the funny voice she used every morning. Finally, Maya stretched and yawned widely before jumping from the window ledge to go outside for her morning ablutions.

The world was waking up at last and Maya's stomach growled, informing her she was ready for some food. Still, she wanted to take a tour around her territory before returning indoors. She disappeared into the undergrowth of the back garden, hiding herself from intruders as she wandered along between the plants. Every now and then, her tabby fur revealed itself as she weaved slowly in and out of the shrubs. She heard a thud off to one side and stopped to listen for more clues as to what had caused the noise. She caught a whiff of a scent – it was another cat. Probably that one from next door who'd been trying to move in on her territory for some time. Her ears twitched as she listened to the other cat's progress through the undergrowth. She was paralysed by indecision. If she stayed still, the other cat would smell her and all hell would break loose; if she moved, there would be a chase and she had no idea how fast the other animal was. She decided to risk staying put to see what happened next.

She caught a glimpse of fur among the plants. It wasn't the grey fur of the cat she was expecting. The markings were more distinctive, another stripy cat like herself, but she didn't recognise the look. Who was it? She stepped cautiously forward, her heart pounding in her chest.

'Maya! Come on, girl!'

The creature hissed and sprinted away, crashing through the undergrowth. Maya was relieved because the last thing she wanted was a fight right at the start of the day, and even worse, one she was bound to lose.

Later that morning, after Sarah had left the house, Maya ventured out again, but this time, she jumped onto the low fence running between her garden and the one next door. She sauntered along it, tail high in the air, looking out for her buddy, Delilah, a sleek, black cat. Maya envied her; her coat was always so glossy and she wished hers looked the same but her stripes seemed to muddy the effect. Dee came bounding towards her across the grass, jumping onto the fence to join her at the last moment. She was so graceful, and as they bumped noses, Maya was glad to have such a good friend living next door.

'How goes it, darling?' she purred before they jumped back into Maya's garden to stretch out in the mid-morning sun.

'I wanted to talk to you about that horrible grey cat who lives behind me. He's such a bully. And there was a different cat skulking around this morning. He almost caught me, but Sarah called out at just the right moment, saving me from another scrap. We really do need to do something.'

Delilah paused in the middle of licking her front leg, already beautifully clean. 'Well, yes, but what? We can't keep other cats out of your garden, can we? Free movement is so important to us all.'

'I agree but I don't want to be terrorised in my own space either.' Maya stood and began pacing back and forth, her dark brown paws looking like velvet as they padded up and down the patio. 'Surely there's something we can do?'

Delilah sat up regally. 'We could gather together the other local cats to see if we can come up with a plan.'

'That sounds like a good idea. I'll try to catch up with as many of them as possible today, and if you do the same, we could meet up later tonight when it gets dark.'

It was agreed and both cats went their separate ways.

Maya returned to the garden just after nightfall. As she passed the corner of the far wall of the house, she saw Delilah waiting for her with about ten other cats from the neighbourhood.

'We can't stop these cats terrorising us all, you know. Unless we can persuade a human to get involved, we don't stand a chance,' said Bob, a grizzly ginger cat who'd seen better days.

'Fat chance of any of them understanding. They're so dim, they'd never pick up on our hints.' Delilah sniffed the air haughtily. A couple of the other cats nodded their agreement. Humans were too unreliable to help.

'What if we could set some kind of trap for the grey cat to run into and close in on it so it couldn't get away?' Maya didn't want to treat another cat this way but she didn't like being threatened either. A sliver of doubt entered her mind as she remembered the different coloured fur of the cat she'd seen that morning.

An almighty screech filled the air. All the undergrowth shook from the obvious fight taking place within it. Bob, the ginger cat jumped down from the wooden table they'd all been sitting on and went a bit closer to investigate. His stubby legs carried him stealthily across the garden. Silence filled the air for a split second until a bullet-shaped streak flew out of the middle of the shrubs and came hurtling towards them, knocking into the ginger cat on its way. It was the grey one from next door, the one they'd been discussing just two minutes earlier.

'Run!' The cat streaked past and on towards the others who were frozen in place on the table watching the unfolding spectacle. He continued on his way, jumping up onto the higher fence on this side of the garden and down into the street.

The other cats turned back to check on Bob, and to see what it was that had frightened the grey cat so much. On the other side of the garden, stood an enormous cat, the like of which they'd never seen before. It looked like a wild cat, with particularly pointed ears and large black tufts of hair on them as well. It didn't seem to have much of a tail either. Its coat was marked like a tabby's but the fur was much thicker, and its paws were enormous. It bared its teeth, making them all shrink back, except for Bob who hadn't moved for quite some time. Maya thought they were all going to die but Sarah chose that moment to open the window and the sound of the television wafted into the garden. The animal turned and disappeared, and a collective sigh of relief echoed across the garden.

'Police have warned householders to be on the lookout for the lynx which escaped from Cranborne zoo yesterday. Although they have searched high and low, they've found no sign of it.'

Maya listened to the television news with only one thought: if only they could tell the humans what they knew.

6

THE LETTER

Juliet sat on the edge of her mother's bed and closed her eyes. It had taken almost every bit of strength she had to come into her mother's bedroom today. She wasn't sure she had any left for the task that lay ahead of her. Gradually, she became accustomed to the musty smell in the air mixed with a faint hint of her mum's usual floral perfume. Tears threatened but she held them at bay. Her right hand gripped the old candlewick bedspread which she had only recently put back on the bed at her mum's insistence when she knew her final days were near. Her eyes sprang open to look at it. She wanted to get rid of it straight away.

That was motivation enough to get her up. She reached out with both hands and pulled the raggedy material towards her, wrinkling her nose as she wondered how long it had been since it had last been washed. Bundling it up, she threw it in a corner ready to go into the washing basket later on. She cast her eye around the rest of the room. It was tidy at least because she'd been coming in every day for weeks now while caring for her mum. She'd kept on top of things but there was just so much to sort out – clothes, jewellery, ornaments – and she hardly knew where to start. She opened the door of the walk-in dressing room and gasped. There were clothes and shoes everywhere, as well as handbags she hadn't seen since she was a child. She fetched a chair from the bedroom and brought it back in so she could climb up and see what else was on the top shelf that ran along the left-hand side of the small room.

As she wasn't tall enough to see what was at the back of the shelf, she let her hands do the work on her behalf. She pulled out the sleeping bags and rucksacks from the front of the shelf, throwing them on to the carpeted floor before stretching forward to see what was lying in the shadows. At first, she couldn't feel anything. She withdrew her hand, grimacing at the dust her fingers had collected while rooting around. She stared at her hands for a matter of seconds before concluding that the only option was to wipe them on her jeans and try not to worry about the mess she was leaving. She stood on her tiptoes to reach forward one last time. And that was when her fingertips landed on the box. Her tongue came out as she applied herself to the task of grasping the box and inching it forward until she could grab hold of it properly and bring it closer. She fell back on to her flat feet and stared at the wooden box in front of her. She recognised it at once. Her mum had called it her box of secrets.

'Everyone has to have one,' her mum used to tell her whenever she asked to see what was inside. 'If I showed you what was in here, it wouldn't be a box of secrets any more, would it?'

As she'd grown older, she'd forgotten all about this box of her mother's. Juliet's forehead wrinkled as she tried to remember how old she'd been when she'd last seen it. Before her dad had left home, she was sure. She'd been only 14 then so over thirty years ago. Now both her parents had passed away, and she could do whatever she wanted. Old habits die hard though and she didn't know if she would be able to summon the courage to go against her mother's wishes. The box was still a forbidden place to her despite her mother's absence. She pulled it towards her, bringing another layer of dust with it, picked it up and stepped carefully down from the chair.

She set the battered box down on her mother's ancient dressing table and pulled out the cushioned stool to sit on. Catching sight of herself in the mirror, she was disconcerted by the number of wrinkles surrounding her eyes. Some were laughter lines, but most were due to the stressful life she led. She wasn't sure she could keep that life up any more. Since her mother had become terminally ill, she had taken a leave of absence from her job at the bank in the city, and she had been surprised to find how little she missed it. Maybe it was time for her to reinvent herself now she had the chance thanks to her mother's will. Her head bobbed as she nodded at herself in confirmation.

The box was still there, calling to her like a mermaid luring her towards danger. 'What was the worst that could happen?' she thought to herself. No-one else was here to see her open the box. No-one would ever know. She reached out and lifted the lid. The box was full of letters bundled together into groups of envelopes each one bound by a red ribbon. Her interest was piqued, and she was suddenly desperate to know who the letters were from. She picked up the first bundle and looked at the postmark. This one had been sent only a year ago. The handwriting was very precise and the ink looked like it had come from a fountain pen. She turned the envelope over but there was no name identifying the sender on the back. She pushed the envelope apart and was surprised to see several folded pages inside. The cream sheets were thick as she pulled them from the envelope and there was a hint of lavender about them as well.

Dear Jean,

Thank you so much for the latest photo of Juliet. I can't believe how beautiful she has become, more so since the last letter even. I do hope that we will get to meet one day.

Juliet turned the pages over to see who had written the letter. It was signed by someone called Colleen. She'd never heard her mum mention a friend with that name. Then she remembered that her mother had kept this letter, and many others, hidden away. Why didn't her mum want her to know Colleen? She continued reading the first page. Colleen had told her mother in great detail about her own three children who all seemed to be a bit younger than Juliet. She was clearly very proud of them all, and a smile flickered across Juliet's face as she took in the things they were doing with their lives.

Sinead is working at the university now, lecturing in French. French of all things! And Niamh is married now with her own baby boy. And Sean has just finished his pilot training. Of course, I've always thought of myself as being the mother of four children, even though I've not been able to live with all of them. I'm so deeply grateful to you for all you've done to keep me as close as I can be to her under the circumstances.

The sheets of paper brushed Juliet's bare legs as they fell to the carpet. Her heart pounded as she tried to make sense of the words she had just read.

The flight to Dublin was a short one giving Juliet little time to think about what was going to happen at the other end. She'd read all the letters Colleen had sent to her mother, which had started even before Juliet was born. She and her mother had both gone to university in Dublin to study Classics and had become firm friends, so when Colleen had fallen pregnant by her then boyfriend and her family had disowned her, Juliet's mother hadn't thought twice about stepping in to help her. Jean had already been married by then and had settled near Manchester.

And just like that, Juliet had discovered a whole new family. She had thought about nothing else since reading the letters between the two women who both thought of themselves as her mother. By the time she had summoned the courage to write her first letter to Colleen, her emotions were completely wrung dry. Both her adoptive parents were now dead, and she would never get the chance to discuss this situation with them. She was glad she had always thought of them as her parents while they were alive though. There was so much she would have liked to ask Jean. Perhaps the issue of her adoption had come between Jean and her husband, pushing him to leave her eventually, and that thought left her wracked with guilt.

As the plane touched down, she tried to focus her mind on the prospect of meeting her biological mother for the first time. All she wanted to do was to know her, and to be known in return; their looks, their shared history, some memories, some family. She grabbed her bag and descended from the plane as quickly as she could, thankful to have been on the same flight as the businessmen coming just for the day. They knew a thing or two about travelling lightly and getting past all the security checks with the minimum delay. Finally, she was on her way to the exit.

She pulled herself up straight and put on a smile. Pushing her tortoiseshell glasses back up her nose, and her long, auburn hair behind her ear, she readied herself to search for the woman she had never heard of until just a few days ago. She was worried that she wouldn't recognise her but as she emerged into the arrivals hall, one woman stood out. Her hair was the same colour as Juliet's, and she was wearing a pair of tortoiseshell glasses. Their eyes locked on to each other and the older woman smiled. Juliet picked up her pace, and it seemed the most natural thing in the world to throw her arms around Colleen when she reached her. She was aware of Colleen doing the same, and suddenly, they were both crying. A long moment passed between them. No words were spoken but so much was said. Finally, they pulled apart to study each other's faces, as if making up for lost time as they imprinted every last detail of mother and daughter into their minds.

'Hello, Colleen, I'm Juliet. It's so wonderful to meet you. We look so much like each other.'

'I know, love. Anyone would think we're related, wouldn't they?'

And the two women laughed as they linked arms and turned to leave the airport. Juliet was sure that Jean was watching them from wherever she was and that she was happy for them to be reunited after all this time.

7

A BRIEF MOMENT OF RESPITE

The first raindrop landed on the windscreen and ricocheted off again, sending tiny droplets of spray into the air. As more drops followed, Cara breathed a sigh of relief, sensing the change in temperature at once. She left her window open as the rain began to pour down, extending her arm outside to feel the cooling water on her skin. There was a beauty to the way it rolled down her hand and on to her fingers before dripping off and landing on the parched ground of the riverbank.

Now it was raining *cats and dogs* as her mum would say and Cara reluctantly closed the window. She started the engine to stop the windscreen steaming up but still, she sat there, unable to bring herself to return. They would be wondering where she'd gone by now but she couldn't face the sense of claustrophobia she felt every time she went back. The river was rising, already approaching the next height marker. Her parents' generation still talked of the time the river had broken its banks but that was many years ago.

Her phone finally buzzed with a message. She was surprised it had taken them so long. No need to read it; she knew what it would say. She switched on the windscreen wipers and reversed out of the riverside car park to navigate the empty, rain-soaked streets that led back to the hospital. The sterile corridors sucked her back in, angry at her for managing to escape their clutches, however briefly. She emerged from the lift on the twelfth floor, her feet taking her back on auto-pilot.

'They're ready to prep you for surgery now, love,' her mum said, taking her hand.

8

_____

CONSUMED

I pulled onto the driveway and switched off the engine but didn't get out of the car. I was dreading what I'd find when I went inside. Sarah had become distant and distracted in recent months spending more and more time on her computer rather than with me. Yet even though I knew that, I still hadn't dared to confront her properly about why. I'd made a couple of half-hearted attempts to talk to her about how the computer was taking over her life but she'd reacted defensively and I was reluctant to provoke another row about it.

The house we shared was eerily silent when I went in at last. I made my way up the stairs to Sarah's study but she wasn't there. I turned around slowly taking in the usual clutter on her desk and in the rest of the room. Nothing seemed out of place. Glancing out of the window, I reassured myself that I had seen Sarah's car on the driveway.

'Sarah!'

I walked along the upper floor checking all the rooms but there was no sign of her. After I'd checked the whole house, I began to worry. There were no messages on my phone from Sarah today, and she had no friends within walking distance. Where could she be?

I retraced my steps back upstairs to her study. Her computer was there, its black screen giving nothing away. I pressed the space bar to see if she'd been working on anything. A document was open showing a single line of text.

'Help me.'

I stared at the words trying to decide whether to go with my instinct and reply. Or was I being ridiculous to think a computer could have sent me a message?

'Who's there?' I typed, instinct taking over.

'Rob, it's me, Sarah.'

'What? Where are you? How are you talking to me?'

'I'm inside the computer. I have a keyboard and screen, and I can see you.'

'But how did you get there? This is crazy.' I pushed my fingers through my hair, wondering if this was all a bad dream.

'I was spending so much time on my computer that I reached a point where I couldn't see where I ended and the machine began. I know that won't make any sense but you were right. I've been consumed.'

'So what happened? One minute you're sitting here at your desk and the next you just disappeared inside the computer.' I laughed refusing to believe this could be true.

'That's exactly how it happened, Rob. I swear I felt my body being sucked in and then I was just in darkness for the longest time before I suddenly appeared here at a new desk but on the other side.'

'But are there other people there or are you alone?'

'There are others here but no-one has spoken to me. They all look as frantic as I feel.'

I fell silent as I pondered the ridiculous magnitude of the situation.

'Rob, are you still there?'

'Yeah, just thinking about how crazy this all is.'

'You will help me, won't you? I should have listened to you. I'm sorry.'

'The last thing I want is for you to be trapped there, wherever there is but I have no idea how to get you out and back here either.'

'I've had an idea about that. I don't know if it will work but it's worth a try.'

After several hours, I'd managed to delete about half the accounts that Sarah had created on her computer. I couldn't believe how many websites she'd signed up to. No wonder she never had any time for me. Then I realised that she'd probably installed a whole load of apps on her phone as well. I stood up and stretched, exhausted both mentally and physically. I cast my eye over the desk looking for Sarah's phone but couldn't see it there so I went in search of it downstairs.

I grabbed a beer from the fridge and sank onto the sofa, picking up Sarah's phone from the side table. Setting the bottle down, I applied myself to getting into the device. Sarah had set up fingerprint access but I swiped up and the number pad appeared. I keyed in the anniversary of our first date, the code she used for everything, and her home page was revealed. Our anniversary was coming up in a few days; I just hoped I could sort this all out by then.

I swiped through the pages and pages of apps shaking my head at just how many she had installed. There were the obvious ones, of course, Facebook, Instagram, Twitter and the like but then there were other more obscure ones that I had no idea why she would have installed on her phone. I glanced from one to the other taking in an app for fashion deals, another for learning languages and even one for a drum pad to make music on the go. To my knowledge, Sarah wasn't at all musical so I was at a loss to understand why she had it.

Then I saw another one called Find Your Soulmate. Intrigued, I clicked on it. It was a dating app. Christ, why would she have one of those? She'd been on it that very morning and had left a conversation visible. I let my finger hover over the tab wondering whether it would be wrong to click. In the end, I couldn't help myself and clicked anyway. She'd been chatting with *sexyhunk123*.

'*Hey, gorgeous. How are you today?*' My mouth dropped open at his opening line.

'*Not bad. How about you? Did you sleep well?*'

'*Yeah, but not as well as I do when you're by my side.*'

I dropped the phone and let out a groan before rubbing my hands over my eyes. My girlfriend of two years, the one I thought was *my soulmate* had been having an affair. The thought of her cheating on me had never even crossed my mind. What a fool I'd been!

I stood up and began pacing back and forth. Would Sarah really have cheated on me? Could I be misreading this? There was only one way to be sure and that was to ask her but something was stopping me from doing that. I bent down to pick up the phone again and checked the app to see where their conversation had ended.

'*Are you still there? Where'd you go?*' was the last thing he'd typed. He had no idea she'd disappeared.

'*I'm back again,*' I typed holding my breath.

'*Busy day?*'

'*Yes, crazy. Wish I was with you right now.*'

'*Well, come round if he's out tonight.*'

'*He's here so I won't be able to get away, but we can keep chatting.*'

'*Let's plan our next date.*'

I stared at the screen and the blinking cursor awaiting my reply. This guy was really familiar with Sarah so it must have been going on for a while. I walked back upstairs to Sarah's office and sat down in front of her computer.

'Hey, Sarah, I'm back.'

'How did you get on?'

'I've moved on to your phone apps now.'

'You have?'

'Yeah, I especially liked that dating app.'

'Oh my God, Rob. There was nothing to it, I swear.'

I didn't even hesitate. I hit CTRL-A then delete, and closed the document. I shut down the computer and left the room.

9

STRANGERS

It all began the day we met when you sat down next to me on the 73 bus trundling north towards Stoke Newington.

'My name's Tom,' you said.

I glanced at you, surprised at your attempt at conversation when we were complete strangers, but I said nothing. I knew the rules and even as an adult, this was definitely against them. But you persisted.

'What's yours?'

'Why?' There was more than a hint of irritation in my voice.

You tutted and I turned away to look out the window. I only had two more stops to go and then I could get away. As soon as we'd gone past the next stop, I stood up and you were forced to stand too. You moved right back, and I only caught your cheeky grin and wink because I couldn't resist one last look at you before leaving. My lips twitched and that's when you knew you had me.

Every day after that, you sat down next to me on the bus on my way home and insisted on talking to me. You asked me every day for a week what my name was until finally, I couldn't take it any more.

'It's Harley.' I waited for the inevitable.

'My dad had a Harley Davidson when I was young. It was his pride and joy.'

I liked the fact that you hadn't just asked me what everyone else always does. So I smiled.

'Mine too.'

And then you smiled.

Soon after, we exchanged numbers and met up for our first proper date. We went to the cinema to see 'Back to the Future' and a month later, we moved in together. As my flat was bigger than yours, you moved in with me.

'This'll be great,' you told me. 'We can share all the bills and everything. It just makes so much more sense.'

We caught the bus together every morning and separated when you got off at Angel to transfer to your job in the City, while I carried on to Euston. I'd never been happier and couldn't wait to introduce you to my family and to meet yours. In fact, that ended up being the cause of our first argument.

'I spoke to my mum today and she invited us round for a barbeque at the weekend.'

'I have to work this weekend but you go.' You didn't even look me in the eye.

'What, you really have to work this weekend?'

Your head snapped up then and there was a look of fury in your eyes. 'As I said, so I can't come.'

'I just want you to meet my family, that's all.'

'For fuck's sake, how many more times?' You slammed your cutlery down on your plate, making the whole thing rattle, pushed back your chair and stomped off to the kitchen.

I'd never seen you angry before and I'd made things worse by questioning you. A few moments later, I heard the front door slam and then there was silence. I didn't know what to think about your behaviour. Hindsight is so much easier after the event. If only I'd known then what was to follow.

You didn't return until the next day by which time, I was frantic with worry but I'd already adapted my behaviour after the night before. I didn't question you and I didn't need to.

'Sorry about last night, babe. I was just annoyed about having to work anyway and I suppose I just felt like you didn't believe me.'

You took me to bed and made it up to me, and the whole incident was pretty much forgotten, except for the niggling doubt in the back of my mind.

Not long after that was the first time you hit me. Once again, I'd made the mistake of questioning you about something minor – an item you'd been unable to find at the supermarket – and the next thing I knew, you'd lashed out with the back of your hand and hit me across the face. The impact was so great that I lost my balance and fell against the wall before sliding to the floor. A second later, you were crouched next to me, full of remorse.

'Oh my God, Harley, I'm so sorry. I don't know what I was thinking. Christ, are you okay?' You gently cradled my face in your hands for a second, looking deep into my eyes. I couldn't understand how you could profess to love me and yet hit me so brutally at the same time. I couldn't bring myself to speak to you. I stood gingerly and took myself off to the bathroom, locking the door behind me. You had the good sense to leave me alone.

I sat down on the toilet seat and hung my head. I had no idea what I could have done to make you start behaving like this. Rather than seeing you as at fault, I was wracked with guilt.

A short while later, after tending to my bruised face, I left the bathroom and made my way back to the kitchen. I wanted to warn you never to hit me again but I was afraid of setting you off. Suddenly, I had no idea what mood you would be in at any given time and that unpredictability filled me with a sense of dread.

Things got back to a kind of normal but I wasn't the same. I didn't feel able to joke and laugh freely around you any more because you might fly off the handle. I started to lose weight, and I found it difficult to sleep. You, meanwhile, seemed to grow in confidence, perhaps even enjoying the sight of my decline.

One day after work when I was on my own at home, my sister, Shelley, turned up on the doorstep out of the blue. I opened the door without even thinking what her reaction might be after not having seen me for a while.

'Christ, Harley! What the hell has happened to you?'

I turned away quickly so she wouldn't see my tears. She followed me inside and made me sit down on the sofa.

'You look ill, you've lost so much weight. What's going on?'

I wanted to explain but once again, I was afraid of the consequences for me if I did.

'I've just been feeling a bit under the weather for a while, that's all.'

'And have you been to the doctor's?'

I shook my head.

'What about Tom? What does he think?' She glanced around as if expecting him to appear.

'I don't know.'

Shelley stared at me in confusion. We were so close. I knew it wouldn't take much for her to work it all out.

'I was worried about you before I came, Harley but now this is worse,' she said, gesturing at me.

The sound of your key in the lock made my heartbeat speed up.

'Please don't say anything,' I told her.

The look in your eyes when you saw Shelley gave me a sinking feeling in the pit of my stomach. I jumped up to greet you.

'Tom, this is... this is my sister, Shelley. She just popped in to see me.'

Shelley stood up and extended her hand. 'Hi, Tom. Good to meet you.'

You didn't reciprocate and for a long moment, the atmosphere in the room was awkward. Then you changed your mind, reaching out to shake Shelley's hand firmly.

'Well, I'd better be on my way and leave you two to your evening,' Shelley announced a minute later. I didn't want her to go. It had been so wonderful to see her. But I also knew that the minute she'd left, you'd start picking on me to cause an argument so you could then justify punishing me.

I showed Shelley to the door.

'Don't be a stranger,' she said before pulling me into a hug. Then she was gone. I closed the door quietly behind her, dreading what was going to happen next.

'What were you talking about with her when she just *popped* in?' You wasted no time in getting in your first dig at me.

'This and that, you know, we haven't seen each other for a while. I didn't know she was coming so it was good to see her.'

'Oh was it? I'm not enough for you now, is that it?' You sneered aggressively at me.

'That's not it. She's my sister and we're very close.'

'Not any more you're not. You'll let her know that she can't come round any more.'

I bit my lip willing myself to stay silent but I couldn't do it.

'I don't want to do that and she won't accept it anyway.'

'What? Are you deliberately going against me?'

You stood up and came towards me. I shrank back against the sofa, afraid of what you would do to me this time. Then you laughed at me.

'It's good that you're afraid of me,' you said softly.

I held my breath waiting for your attack. It was only a matter of time. You'd gone very still and then suddenly, you lunged for me and grabbed my hair, pulling me to standing using only my hair to help you. My scalp was screaming from the pain and hot tears fell down my cheeks. Then you started shouting in my face.

'You don't deserve me. You're just a worthless, lying bitch. I know you asked her over here to moan about me. Well, that's never going to happen again, do you hear?' You yanked hard on my hair and then hit me in the face once more. I landed with a thud on the sofa and something inside me snapped. I glanced to the side of me to see what was there that I could use to protect myself. As you advanced towards me again, I grabbed the vase of flowers I'd placed on the side table earlier and hit you over the head with it repeatedly until you slumped onto the floor. When I was sure you weren't able to hurt me any more, I stood up and grabbed my phone. I called 999 and then I called Shelley. I kept hold of the vase in case you came to.

The police came and took you away bringing my nightmare to an end. As I sipped the sweet tea Shelley had made me, I thought back to the day we'd met. I never knew what sort of monster you really were when you were charming me back then. Maybe I should have just followed my instincts and not let myself get involved with a stranger after all. My only hope now was that I would never see you again.

10

FROM A BYGONE AGE

'What will happen to them all, Josie?'

Josie turned her wrinkled face towards her friend and frowned. 'What do you mean?'

'After we've gone, I mean. Who'll point out to them the dangers they're facing?'

'Oh, I see. Well, our children will have to take on their share of the responsibility. And many of them are already doing that. We can see that for ourselves today. We can trust them.'

'But can we really, Josie? Look at how so many people chose to vote in that referendum. I never thought I'd live to see the day.'

'We've lived through worse, Bert, and we're here to tell the tale.'

'They've never had to live through a world war like we did but if things carry on like this, they might end up doing that after all.'

'God forbid.' Josie crossed herself, briefly closing her eyes to block out the awful memories of that time.

They linked arms as the crowd moved forward. Josie lifted her banner higher, every bit as enthusiastic as the other younger protesters surrounding her. Bert strode forward, his walking stick providing the balance his fragile body could no longer manage.

They were approaching Parliament Square now and Josie was hopeful they would find a bench somewhere to sit down while they listened to the speakers who were coming that day. A few minutes later, they found one with some younger people occupying it but as soon as they saw Josie and Bert, they jumped up to let them take their places.

'Thank you kindly,' said Bert. 'That's very good of you.'

The young people smiled and moved away.

'Do you think all this will make any difference?' Bert waved his stick around at the protesters.

'It has to, Bert, just like it did in the war. We stood up for what we believed in then and that's just what we're doing now. If we don't protest, then we'll only have ourselves to blame when it all goes wrong.'

'Aye, you're right, Josie. It just feels like we valued our freedom more in those days, and we knew what being free really meant. Nowadays, I'm not sure everyone does.'

'Times have changed though, Bert. People value different things now. They're more material in many ways. It's sad how much stuff some of us have and yet more people are living in poverty than ever before.'

'And that's when fascism is at its most dangerous just like we found out back then. People are always looking for someone to blame and it always seems to be immigrants who are on the receiving end of that hatred as you know only too well.'

Josie rubbed at the tattoo on her wrist. She'd lost everything and yet she'd found a new home here. She couldn't face losing it all again, and that's why she was here today. History must not repeat itself. If it was the last thing she did, she would try and make sure of that.

11

NEW HORIZONS

'Would you like me to accompany you in the car, Mrs. Phillips?'

'No, thank you, Jacobs, that will not be necessary.'

The butler bowed and left the room. Valerie glanced out through the conservatory windows to her beloved garden. She still couldn't quite accept that Carlton was gone. She was dreading today and would have liked some company in the car, but it wouldn't do to let her butler be her companion for a day like this. She had hoped that at least one of Carlton's children would have offered to travel with her but despite all her efforts, she was no closer to them now after ten years of trying than she had been on her wedding day.

She looked down at her half-eaten breakfast and, unable to eat any more, she laid her napkin next to her plate and stood up. She smoothed down her black dress and with a final longing glance at the garden, she left to collect the rest of her things from the hallway. As Jacobs was helping her into her jacket and coat, the black hearse arrived outside the front door. A shudder went through her at the thought of her husband's lifeless body lying inside that coffin. He was to be buried in the family plot after the service – he had been adamant about that – which was yet another tradition she had never quite accustomed herself to. She wanted to be cremated. Once her soul was gone, she couldn't see the point of burying her bones in the ground.

A light rain began to fall as she slipped into the back seat of the car. The black clouds dominated the sky, making an already gloomy day even more unappealing. The short journey from the manor house to the local church seemed to take longer than usual, as though everything was happening in slow motion. They passed children playing in the school playground, people milling around the village shop, others going about their morning routines, but as the hearse went by, they all stopped to stare for a moment, to wonder about the unfortunate person inside the coffin, and what had brought about their death.

The car pulled up outside the church where several guests were already waiting for the service to begin. She could see Carlton's sons, Joseph and Stephen, waiting to take their place as pall-bearers. Ashen-faced, they were vulnerable figures standing in the rain ready to do their duty for their father.

The driver of the hearse opened Valerie's door and she stepped out onto the gravel drive and into the shelter of the umbrella he was holding above her. She took the umbrella and turned towards the path leading to the church's arched entrance.

'Joseph, Stephen,' she acknowledged both men softly as she passed, receiving curt nods back from them both but no words or gestures of comfort. She understood their pain – Carlton's death at such a young age had taken them all by surprise – but their refusal to accept her into their lives still cut her deeply after all this time. She had never tried to fill their mother's shoes, but they treated her as though she had as if they blamed her for their mother's death from cancer so many years ago.

As she approached the church, she saw Annabel, Carlton's daughter waiting at the entrance. Annabel had softened towards her over the years, but when Valerie reached her hand out towards her, the younger woman turned away without a word to enter the church. Valerie found herself rooted to the spot by the unexpected rejection. Tears sprang to her eyes. She would have given anything for a child of her own to share this burden with now.

'Valerie, are you all right?' She looked up into the worried face of Carlton's brother, George. She gave him a wobbly smile, unable to find any words to convey her emotions. He took her arm and walked with her down the aisle towards the altar. The front row was full on both sides, with no space left for her to take her place as Carlton's wife. George guided her gently into the second row, next to his wife, who she had become very close to during her married life.

'Come and sit next to me, my dear,' Angela said. 'How are you holding up?'

'I'm fine, really,' she replied, grateful for their kind words. She sat down on the pew, her back straight and her head held high, refusing to let her step-children know just how much she was grieving.

Through the service, she listened to Carlton's children talk about him and their mother with fond memories. She heard their gratitude for the faith he had put in them in recent years, when he had handed the reins of the family business over to them completely.

This had at least allowed him to spend more time with Valerie, a blessing for which she would be eternally thankful.

It was only when George went to speak that any mention was made of her at all, much to the obvious irritation of the three children. George spoke of how much fun they'd all enjoyed as doubles partners at the tennis club, and on their shared travels to Europe and further afield. Valerie smiled as she thought of their house in the south of France, and the many happy holidays they'd spent there. Carlton had lived a life of luxury as a result of inheriting his father's wealth and his estate, and she had been lucky enough to enjoy it too, as his wife.

And that was what the children were worried about – who was going to inherit it all now?

She didn't linger at the graveside. She was desperate to get away.

'Goodbye George, Angela. Thanks for making this bearable for me.' She kissed them both on the cheek.

'We'll see you at Joe's place,' George replied.

'No... I haven't been invited, and that's fine. I'm going home now.' George's face fell but she wasn't upset. She just wanted to be gone.

Back at the house, she was pleased to see that her car had been brought round to the front in her absence, and as Jacobs let her back in, that her bags were in the hallway.

'Please could you put my bags in the car, Jacobs, while I go and change?'

'Of course, madam.'

She changed quickly into something more comfortable for her journey, cast her eye around her bedroom one last time, and went quickly back downstairs.

'Thank you so much for all your hard work, Jacobs. I wish you luck.' She gave him the envelope she'd been keeping and made her way to her car. As she drove to the airport, she smiled at the thought that in a few short hours, she would be back in the south of France in her new home. Carlton had put the house and its estate in her name the previous year.

'Just in case, darling,' he'd said.

That was all she needed to remember him by. They could have the rest.

12

SAVED BY THE BOOKSHOP

Emma stepped down from the train and was immediately jostled along the platform by all the other impatient passengers. When a storage area appeared up ahead, she scooted off to one side, relieved to escape the crowds. She tried to remember the last time she'd taken a train anywhere, let alone been among so many people. Inhaling a deep breath, she relaxed her shoulders, brushed her dark hair out of her eyes and wished once again she'd had her hair cut before coming for this job interview. She peeked out of her hiding place a few minutes later and, seeing the platform was now virtually empty, set off towards the exit.

Emerging on to the street, her eyes were drawn to the large black clouds overhead. She berated herself for leaving home without a raincoat or umbrella, especially when she still had an hour to kill before the interview. The last thing she wanted was to turn up looking like a drowned rat. She'd worn her only suit to make sure she was giving the best impression she could, leaving them no choice but to give her the job. After a quick check of the bus departure times for the university campus, she set off into town for a wander. As her high-heeled feet stumbled on the cobblestones, memories from her university days came rushing back and with them, a need to return here permanently, as an employee, not a student. The streets weren't quite as familiar as they'd been a few years ago; a lot of the shops were new and not especially inviting to her quiet, librarian's mind.

A crack of thunder sounded above, a sure sign that rain would follow. She ducked into the first shop entrance and her face lit up when she noticed the sign. The bell tinkled as she pushed the door open but when she closed it behind her, there was only silence; a silence she knew and loved well. Her delight at the endless books displayed before her was almost overwhelming. After a minute she moved to study the bookshelves. She'd just finished a book on the train and hoped to find another one for her return. Her tastes were varied but she was in the mood for a romance next. So many of the larger bookstores didn't even bother with a romance section. 'Why not?' she wanted to ask. Her eyes landed on the sign announcing the start of the romance section just a heartbeat later, and all at once, she fell in love with the little shop.

'Are you looking for something particular?' A deep voice resonated just behind her, so close she could almost feel it. She whirled round to be met by the sight of a man so handsome she wasn't quite sure if he was real. She took in his dark brown, curly hair matched to his chocolate-coloured eyes and the smattering of stubble on his jawline. She swallowed nervously, words failing her. When she didn't speak, his eyebrows went up ever so slightly and a quirky smile overtook his face.

'Erm...' she managed, feeling her face flush. She coughed lightly and tried again. 'I've just finished my book, and was looking for a new one, perhaps a romance.' Her voice had softened to a whisper by the time she'd finished. He leaned towards her, making her heart beat a bit faster, but then swerved around her to pull out a colourful book from the shelf. She recognised the author's name as he turned the book over so she could read the blurb. His long, slim fingers brushed hers as he handed it to her, sending a jolt of electricity through her whole body.

'This one's just in,' he said as he turned back towards his desk to answer the phone. He spoke confidently into the receiver, revealing himself as the owner. He glanced down at his watch, and she suddenly realised she'd forgotten the time. He looked up straight into her eyes and, seeing her standing there, book in hand, hurried to bring his call to an end. Emma mirrored his gesture, glancing at her own watch; she was in danger of being late if she didn't get going soon. She wanted to stay, browse the shelves and maybe get to know the bookstore owner better. In other circumstances, she might have been bold for once but she really needed this job.

'Can I take this one please?' she asked as soon as he put the phone down. She handed him the money, grabbed the book and, with a quick but anxious smile, dashed off but not before she noticed the surprised expression on his face.

Thankfully, the bus stop was just along the street, and after a minute's wait, she caught the bus to the university. She sank into the seat nearest the door and breathed a sigh of relief. But her mind kept returning to the bookshop owner's face when she'd run out. She shook her head, needing to focus before the job interview. A lot was riding on it, not least that she had hardly any money left since being made redundant from the town library when the council had closed it down in its latest money-saving scheme. The residents of her little Yorkshire town had fought the decision but in the end, it was all in vain. It hadn't been a well-paid job but she'd loved it.

The bus pulled up near the familiar red brick building of the university library on the opposite corner. This was a more modern library than the one in the city centre but she didn't mind. The job was the most important thing and it would be a promotion for her too. Thank goodness the rain had held off. She smoothed down her suit and pasted her practised look of self-confidence onto her face.

Barely an hour later, she climbed back on to the bus with a heavy heart. She'd loved the sound of the job and the interview had gone well but she was convinced the other candidates were all much better qualified than her. She went straight back to the station to catch the next train. If she wasn't going to get the job of her dreams, she didn't want to go back to the bookshop to see the owner again. It was best just to go home and get on with looking for another job there.

As Tom was locking up at the end of a busy day, settling down to deal with a mountain of paperwork, the beautiful girl who'd run out of the shop earlier came back to him in all her stunning glory: long, wavy brown hair nestling on her slight shoulders; the greenest eyes he'd ever seen, like the emerald sea he remembered from childhood holidays to Mediterranean islands; and she had a calm presence about her which was both reassuring and attractive. When his fingers had brushed hers, he'd been taken aback to feel the connection between them. He hadn't experienced that feeling with anyone in a very long time.

And then she was gone. What had he done to make her leave in such a hurry? He shrugged to himself and sighed, forcing himself to focus on the papers before him. He'd been running the bookshop for three years now since leaving university and although it was doing well considering the competition from the big high street names, it was a constant slog to keep on top of things on his own. He couldn't afford any staff and he was open six days a week, leaving little time to sort out orders of new stock or to keep his accounts up-to-date. Still, he had nothing else going on in his life so he just got on with it. He worked solidly for an hour before closing down his laptop and locking up the shop to make his way home.

As the bus inched along the main road out of the city, he turned his thoughts to the book club's next meeting just two weeks away. His sister helped him because the meetings were usually busy and the crowd was an opinionated one, which he found difficult to manage, especially as he hardly ever had time to read the chosen book. That was the downside he had to put up with: his sister chose the books and her choice was very conservative. He couldn't think how to persuade her to allow a variety of genres without her taking offence on behalf of the literary tomes she loved so much. Still, the crowds kept coming. They were all his regular customers as well and that was enough to persuade him to let the book club continue.

He got off the bus but crossed over the road to pop into the university library on his way home. He loved coming back here where he'd spent so many hours studying for his degree, even if it was only to put up a flyer for his book club meetings. They were happy for him to do so, especially as he offered a discount to all university students during their course.

'Hey, Tom, how's it going?' He turned round to see his former flatmate, Ed, standing in front of him.

'I'm great, Ed, thanks. How about you?' Tom closed the flap on his messenger bag as Ed started to tell him all his news.

Walking back down the corridor a short while later, he thought about how much Ed had changed since leaving university. He was a go-getter type, hardly starting one job before thinking about what he wanted to aim for next. He'd only been the Library Manager for a couple of years and now he was taking the next step up to be a Director of the Library. He wondered absently what the new manager would be like and hoped they would continue to work with him in the future.

Emma broke down the last of her boxes and put it next to the recycling bin along with the others she'd used to transport her belongings north after getting the job at the library. She'd hired a small van on Friday morning to drive up the motorway to her new home and had spent the rest of the day unpacking before dropping the van off in the city and catching the bus back home. She'd been lucky to find a one-bedroom flat to rent near her new workplace, and although it was small, it was hers, and her neighbours were professionals just like her. She would keep to herself for the most part anyway. She did have plans to get to know one person better now she'd got the job and could see a future for herself here. And she'd already found the perfect opportunity.

An hour later, Emma got off the bus back in the city centre and made her way to the bookshop. She hovered outside suddenly nervous about her plan to join the book club meeting tonight when she knew no-one else. She'd found out about it courtesy of a poster on the university library notice board when she'd popped in the day before to sort out her new office. Now she just felt presumptuous. What if he was married or in a relationship? She began to turn away, self-doubt creeping back in and overtaking her fragile confidence.

'Hello, have you come for the book club meeting?' that familiar deep voice asked once again, the doorbell tinkling behind him. She had no choice but to turn back and face up to her plans.

'Hello,' she replied simply.

The bookstore owner smiled. 'We've met before, haven't we? I'm Tom by the way.' He held the door open and she walked inside, coming to a stop by his desk.

He looked expectantly at her, waiting for her reply. She took a deep breath. 'I'm Emma. I came in a couple of weeks ago but had to leave very quickly.'

He frowned, his mind seeming to whirr. 'Got it! You bought a romance book, I think.' She nodded with a surprised smile. 'Yes, I remember you were in a bit of a hurry. Shame that.' He gave her a glorious, dimpled grin and she thought her knees might give way.

'I had a job interview that day,' she explained, 'and I realised I was running a bit late.'

'Did you get it then? The job, I mean.' He'd started putting chairs out in a circle and she picked the next one up ready to help. His hand brushed hers again as he took the chair from her and he stopped to stare at her.

'Yes, I start work at the university library on Monday.'

Tom's face lit up. 'Excellent. My friend Ed did the job before you and we worked together so I should be seeing more of you then.'

Just then a very pretty girl appeared from a back room and Emma's heart sank. This must be his girlfriend and the end of her little fantasy.

'Tom, do you want me to get the urn going?' She looked at Emma and smiled briefly before returning her attention to Tom, her long, blonde hair swaying at the speed of the movement.

'Yes, please. George, this is Emma. She's new in town and is joining us for the first time tonight.'

'Oh, welcome,' she said breezily. 'Have you read the book we're discussing tonight?'

Emma nodded, unable to speak, the weight of her disappointment hanging heavily over her.

'Even better. At least you and I will know what we're talking about, unlike my brother here. I don't know, he runs a bookshop with a book club and hasn't even found time to read the book.' Emma's head snapped up to look at Tom and he winked at her, making her blush as she realised that he'd probably guessed what she'd been thinking about.

'That's what I have you here for, George. Anyway, Emma is the new university librarian so I imagine she knows a thing or two about books.'

'Well, I'm really glad you could come, Emma. It will make a nice change to have a true book-lover here.' She turned away with a flounce to go and sort out the urn, leaving Tom and Emma alone again.

'I'm glad you came this evening too, Emma,' Tom told her. 'I hope this will be the start of a long relationship between you and the bookshop.'

'It won't be the first time that I've been saved by a bookshop,' she replied, as she took her seat next to him ready for the meeting to begin and for the next phase of her life with it.

THE END

Because reviews are vital in spreading the word, please leave a brief review on **Amazon** if you enjoyed reading *Bittersweet - 12 Short Stories for Modern Life*. Thank You!

READ AN EXTRACT OF FROM HERE TO NASHVILLE

POOLE, DORSET, ENGLAND

Rachel

'It's time for our last session of the evening now, folks. We're proud to present to you the next big thing in UK country music. Please give it up for local band Three's Company!'

The crowd applauded in response and I took a deep breath to try and stop my heart from racing as I walked over to the microphone. It didn't matter how many gigs we did, I still felt nervous every time. With a quick glance round I checked that Sam, the guitarist, and Matt, the drummer, were ready. I tossed my hair over my shoulder and moved my guitar into position, running my fingers gently over the strings to reassure myself before the growing audience.

The boys played the opening bars of Lady Antebellum's 'Need You Now' and I relaxed, letting my voice take over and lead the way. As the song ended, the crowd gave another good round of applause so we went straight on to our second number. About halfway through, I spotted a man watching me intently. He was tall, with broad shoulders and he had a healthy-looking tan. His dark brown hair curled invitingly around his face and his jaw was covered by a fine layer of stubble. He smiled encouragingly so he didn't put me off my stride and reluctantly I looked away. But I was intrigued.

By the end of the song, the crowd was singing along. More and more people had started to come in, drawn by the sound of our music, which boosted our confidence still further so I felt the time was right for some introductions.

'Hi, we're Three's Company and it's great to be here tonight.' I had to pause and wait for the cheers to subside. Smiling, I carried on, 'I'd like to take a minute to introduce the band. Sam's on guitar and that's his brother, Matt, on drums.' They both grinned and gave a little wave. 'I'm Rachel and next up, is a song of mine called "My Turn".'

I settled myself on the stool at the front of the stage, making sure I was comfortable before playing the introduction so that I could focus and get my first public performance of this song perfect. I'd written it with my mum in mind and I only wished she could see me sing it now.

'All my life, I've been waiting, waiting for my turn,
Wondering how much longer it's gonna be...
And when it comes, I'm gonna make sure I take it,
Make the most of it, live my turn to the limit.'

I didn't look up until I reached the end of the song and when I finished singing, there was complete silence in the pub, feeding my fears for a brief moment. This was swiftly followed by thunderous applause though and I could not believe the crowd's reaction.

When we broke for the interval, I rushed to hug Sam and Matt, flushed with our success. Standing at the crowded bar a few minutes later with my heart still pounding and a huge smile on my face, I suddenly felt the hairs stand up on the back of my neck.

I turned slowly to find myself staring up into the most beautiful pair of brown eyes I'd ever seen. The gorgeous man who'd been watching me earlier now stood before me and my breath caught as I studied him close up. He towered over my petite frame, his soft, wavy, dark brown hair falling over his forehead, hands slung low in his pockets and cowboy boots peeking out from beneath his jeans.

'Er, hi,' I managed to stutter out, reminding myself to breathe.

'Hey there,' he drawled in the most luscious American accent. 'I heard you singing and I wanted to find out more about who that fabulous voice belonged to.' He smiled and as he did, I noticed the way his lips turned up invitingly at the corners.

'Thank you. I'm glad you liked it,' I replied, trying to appear calm and to bring my focus back to his eyes.

And then he chuckled. God, he knew how to make a chuckle sound sexy. He oozed confidence too, with his broad shoulders pulled back and his head held high.

'You British, you're so damn polite,' he said, raising his eyebrows. 'You sounded great up there.'

'Yeah, the crowd had a great vibe tonight. I can't quite believe it.'

'Well, you have no reason not to; the proof's all here. I loved your own song by the way. You have a real talent there.'

I blushed then, an honest-to-goodness shade of pink that made him chuckle once more, locking eyes with me as he did, so I knew the compliment was sincere.

'I'd love to hear more of your singing. Have y'all any more gigs coming up?'

'We've got another one next Tuesday at a local pub down on the quayside. Do you know where that is?'

I gave him a cheeky smile, feeling like I'd somehow been transported to an alternate universe where I flirted with handsome Americans all the time, and he rewarded me with a playful grin by return. Wow! His grin was almost sinful. I didn't know how much longer my legs would support me, after the excitement of being on stage and now this unfamiliar feeling of attraction. I took a step back and reached out to hold on to the bar behind me.

'Well, I'm staying with my cousin, Tom. He's the bartender here so I'm sure he'll help me get to the *quayside*, whatever that is.' He tilted his head to one side endearingly and frowned a little as he considered the possibilities.

'It's down at the waterfront.' I smiled again, picking up on his confusion. 'Tom lives a couple of doors away from me actually so he knows how to get to most places.'

'Great, I'll look forward to it. I'm Jackson by the way, Jackson Phillips.' He held out his hand towards me.

'Rachel Hardy,' I responded, placing my hand in his. The warmth of his skin against mine set my pulse racing once more, as he held my hand and my gaze for what seemed like an eternity.

By this time, Tom had made it over to us. 'What can I get you two to drink?' he asked, bringing us both back to reality. 'Fantastic set, Rachel, by the way. The crowd loved it.'

I asked for a lime and soda, as did Jackson. When Tom brought the drinks back a moment later, Jackson insisted on paying for them and I took a long sip while I collected my thoughts.

'Where are you from then, Jackson?' I turned to face him and found him already looking at me, with that intensity that had caught my attention when I was singing.

'I'm from Nashville. Do you know it?'

I coughed and spluttered as I tried to swallow the sip of drink I had taken at just the wrong time. He reached out to pat me on the back, looking concerned by my reaction.

'You okay?'

'Sorry,' I managed, 'it's just that was the last thing I expected you to say. I've always dreamed of going to Nashville.' I could only hope that my face didn't have a silly teenage look on it.

'Well, it's good to have a dream to work towards and I can heartily recommend it to you. I'm over here for Tom's wedding to Meg at the end of the month, I'm going to be his best man.'

As I cast my eyes over his perfectly toned body, a sudden wicked vision of Jackson in a morning suit appeared before me. I must have given myself away because he was now looking at me quite differently. My face warmed under his scrutiny. Thankfully, my best friend, Jenna, chose that moment to come over and introduce herself.

'Rachel, found you at last!' She pulled me in for a quick hug, forcing me to tear my attention away from Jackson for a moment. 'You guys sounded brilliant out there. All those practice gigs over the last few years have paid off, you know. I felt really proud of you all, even those two brothers of mine.'

'We did a pretty good job tonight, didn't we?' I admitted before turning back to Jackson. 'Jenna, this is Jackson Phillips, he's Tom's cousin and he's over here from *Nashville*.' I raised my eyebrows slightly, knowing she would get the connection. They said hello and then I had to down my drink quickly because it was time for me to get back to the stage.

I cast a final look in Jackson's direction and he tilted his head gently towards me, giving me another charming smile. His gaze followed me all the way to the stage and the attention made my stomach flutter.

We started the second half with our version of 'Killing Me Softly With His Song', keeping quite faithfully to Roberta Flack's original, before going on to some other covers, including 'This Kiss' by Faith Hill.

All too soon, I sat down at the piano to introduce our final number. I'd chosen another one of my own songs to finish with, called 'Don't Let Me Go'.

'How can things have turned out like this?
I thought you'd be here forever
But now you've gone and I'm on my own.
I couldn't make you stay but promise me one thing
Don't let me go...'

The crowd cheered their approval for this final song. People came up for some time afterwards to congratulate us on our success before going on their way. Finally, only Jackson remained, smiling at me and waiting for me to finish receiving all the compliments. Sam and Matt had already started taking the gear out to the van so it took a few minutes before I could introduce them to him.

'Sam, Matt, meet Jackson, Tom's cousin. He's over here from America for Tom's wedding.'

'Whereabouts in America are you from?' asked Sam, as he put his guitar carefully back into its case.

'Nashville,' Jackson explained.

'As in, Nashville, Tennessee, Music City,' I reinforced.

'Yep, the very same,' Jackson laughed. 'That's how I know you guys sound so good. I've heard a few bands in my time,' he said.

'Nice to meet you and thanks,' Sam replied, shaking Jackson's hand.

'Hello, Jackson, glad you enjoyed the gig,' Matt said, a bit breathless after packing his drums away. 'Rachel, sorry to interrupt but do you want a lift home?' he continued. 'Jenna's waiting in the van.'

'No, I'll walk back as it's such a lovely evening, but thanks anyway.'

'If you only live a couple of doors away from Tom, I can walk you back to make sure you get home safely, if that's okay with you, Rachel,' Jackson offered, looking first at me and then at Sam and Matt as if he knew they acted as my protectors.

'Is that okay with you, Rachel?' asked Sam. The sullen look on his face caught me off-guard. I was used to him being protective of me in the absence of a brother of my own, but this wasn't the same and I couldn't quite put my finger on it.

'Yes, of course,' I said, pushing my worries away. 'Thank you, Jackson and thanks guys, for an awesome performance tonight. I'll call you tomorrow for a post-gig analysis!' I gave them both a hug and a kiss and they turned to leave.

I looked at Jackson and blew out a long, slow breath.

'A penny for your thoughts?' he asked.

That made me laugh, to hear this typically English phrase coming out of his mouth. I studied his face for a moment.

'I'm not quite sure what to make of you. I've never met anyone from Nashville before and you're taking me a bit by surprise.'

'And that's a good thing, right?' His eyes twinkled. 'Shall we go?'

Jackson took my guitar for me and we walked back slowly along the quay, delighting in all the sparkling lights and the buzz from the tourists out enjoying meals on the warm summer evening. Once or twice, his hand brushed mine as we walked and I wondered if he felt the same tingling sensation I did every time our skin touched.

'Have you always enjoyed singing?' he asked.

'Oh yes, since I was young, my mum and dad encouraged it. We always had music in the house.'

'And were your parents there tonight?' he asked.

For a moment, I couldn't answer. 'My parents have both passed away,' I whispered and found myself stopping in the street.

He took my hand.

'I'm really sorry. Sorry that happened to you and for being nosy.' He groaned.

'Don't worry. It was a natural question to ask and I don't mind talking about them.'

We started walking again and he let go of my hand. I missed the warm, reassuring feel of it.

'Did they ever hear you and the band sing?'

'No, they didn't get the chance.'

'Well, they sure would have been proud of you tonight.'

To my relief, he didn't ask me how they'd died. My family's past was my burden and not something I chose to talk about very often.

Before I knew it, we'd reached my gate and it was time to say goodbye but there was still so much I wanted to say.

'Your next gig is on Tuesday, you said. What's the name of the pub?'

'It's called The Cork and Bottle and we'll be on at eight again. I'll have to make sure we play some different songs then if you might be coming,' I joked.

'I'll definitely be there.'

My heart flipped over at his confident reply.

'Great, it will be good to see you again.' I paused, uncertain of what to say next. 'Well, I enjoyed meeting you tonight, Jackson,' I said, looking up at him one last time, 'and thank you for walking me home.' I reached out to touch him lightly on the arm, letting my hand linger for a moment before pulling away.

'The pleasure was all mine. Goodnight,' he replied softly, his deep voice caressing me right till the very last minute. Then, he handed me back my guitar, turned and continued on his walk home.

Watching him go, I had the feeling that my life had just taken a turn for the better.

ALSO BY JULIE STOCK

From Here to You series

Before You - Prequel - From Here to You

From Here to Nashville - Book 1 - From Here to You

Over You - Book 2 - From Here to You

Finding You - Book 3 - From Here to You

From Here to You series

Domaine des Montagnes series

First Chance - Prequel - Domaine des Montagnes

The Vineyard in Alsace - Book 1 - Domaine des Montagnes

Starting Over at the Vineyard in Alsace - Book 2 - Domaine des Montagnes

A Leap of Faith at the Vineyard in Alsace - Book 3 - Domaine des Montagnes

Standalone

The Bistro by Watersmeet Bridge

ABOUT THE AUTHOR

Julie Stock writes contemporary feel-good romance from around the world: novels, novellas and short stories.

She published her debut novel, *From Here to Nashville*, in 2015, after starting to write as an escape from the demands of her day job as a teacher. *A Leap of Faith at the Vineyard in Alsace* is her latest book, and the third in the Domaine des Montagnes series set on a vineyard.

Julie is now a full-time author, and loves every minute of her writing life. When not writing, she can be found reading, her favourite past-time, running, a new hobby, or cooking up a storm in the kitchen, glass of wine in hand.

Julie is a member of The Society of Authors.

Julie is married and lives with her family in Cambridgeshire in the UK.

Sign up for Julie's free author newsletter at **www.julie-stock.co.uk.**

ACKNOWLEDGMENTS

I wrote these stories in 2018 when I took part in a story writing challenge run by 12shortstories.com. The challenge was to write a new short story every month to a different prompt and a specific word count.

It was a great challenge because it really helped me to master the art of the short story which is so different to writing a novel. I also enjoyed the excitement every month of seeing what the new prompt was and how tight the word count was.

I would like to thank the other authors who took part in the challenge for their constructive criticism every month and for creating such a great sense of community around the challenge.

I'd also like to thank the Beta Buddies, a group of author friends, some of whom had the time to read these stories as well and to give me their feedback before publication.

Finally, I'd like to send a huge thank you to my fledgling group of advanced readers, who were the last group of people to read these stories before publication. I'm so grateful for their comments and for the time they gave so generously to me.

Printed in Great Britain
by Amazon